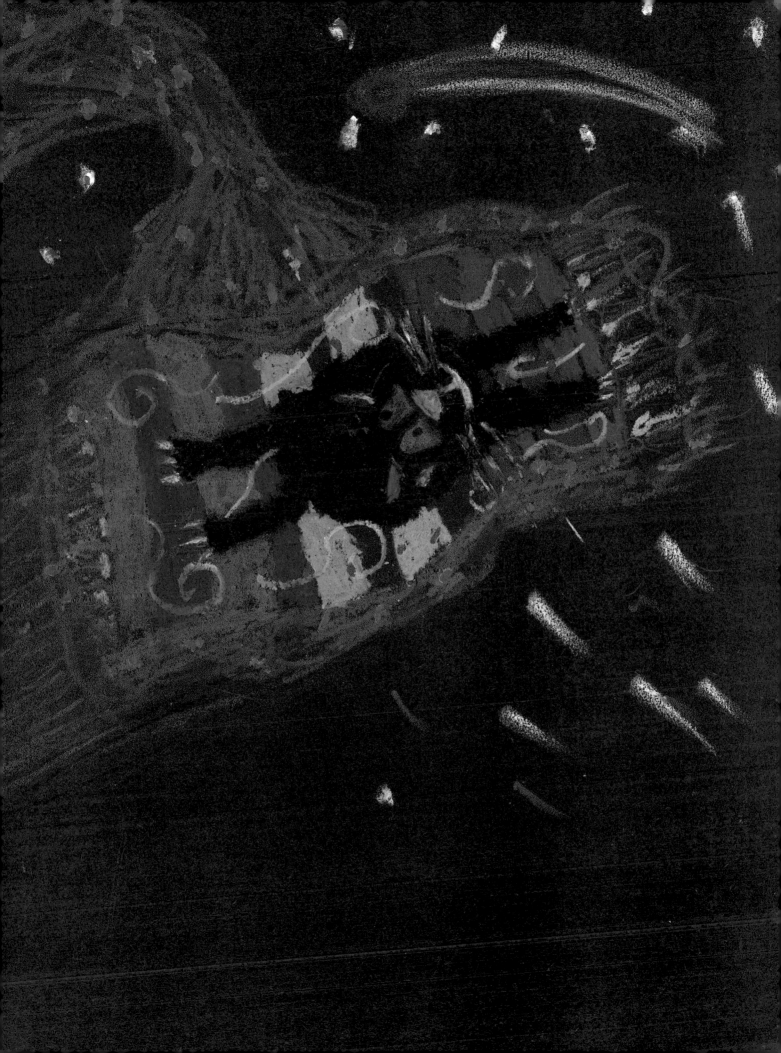

Front endpapers by Freya Elsy aged 11
Back endpapers by Fraser McGregor aged 8
Thank you to Neston Primary School, Neston, Wiltshire
for helping with the endpapers – K.P.
For Maya, who will soon be able to read this – V.T.
For Julia Moxley – K.P.

OXFORD
UNIVERSITY PRESS

Great Clarendon Street, Oxford OX2 6DP

Oxford University Press is a department of the University of Oxford.
It furthers the University's objective of excellence in research, scholarship,
and education by publishing worldwide in

Oxford New York

Auckland Cape Town Dar es Salaam Hong Kong Karachi
Kuala Lumpur Madrid Melbourne Mexico City Nairobi
New Delhi Shanghai Taipei Toronto

With offices in

Argentina Austria Brazil Chile Czech Republic France Greece
Guatemala Hungary Italy Japan Poland Portugal Singapore
South Korea Switzerland Thailand Turkey Ukraine Vietnam

Oxford is a registered trade mark of Oxford University Press
in the UK and in certain other countries

British Library Cataloguing in Publication Data available

ISBN: 978-0-19-275574-2 (paperback)

Printed in Italy

Paper used in the production of this book is a natural, recyclable product made
from wood grown in sustainable forests. The manufacturing process conforms to the
environmental regulations of the country of origin

CONGRATULATIONS!
To Matilda Snook, winner of the
Winnie's Midnight Dragon competition,
who appears in this book
along with her winning dragon drawing.
Look out for them both in the pictures!

www.korkypaul.com

Winnie's Flying Carpet

Valerie Thomas and Korky Paul

OXFORD
UNIVERSITY PRESS

Winnie the Witch was busy
writing letters.

They were thank-you letters
for her birthday presents.

Now there was only one left, the trickiest letter.
Winnie's sisters, Wilma, Wanda, and Wendy,
had given her a flying carpet.
Winnie had always wanted a flying carpet.
But *this* flying carpet had been a disappointment.

Actually, it had been a disaster.

Dear Wilma,
Wanda, and Wendy,
thank you very much
for the

There was the time it got tangled
in Winnie's washing.

And the day it tipped over as they were passing a duck pond.

And then one day it turned a corner too quickly.

After that, Winnie rolled up the carpet, tied it with string . . .

put it in the broom cupboard, and locked the door.

But Winnie wanted to write something *nice* about the carpet in her thank-you letter.

She unlocked the cupboard, untied the carpet, and spread it on the armchair.

It is a beautiful carpet, she thought. It seems a pity not to use it.

So Winnie decided to give it one more chance.

Just then, the door bell rang.

Ding! Dong!

Winnie hurried off to answer it . . .

just as Wilbur came inside.

After a busy morning climbing trees and chasing butterflies, he was ready for a sleep.

The sun was shining on the flying carpet. It looked so warm and comfortable. Wilbur jumped up and in one minute he was snoring.

The flying carpet waited
one more minute.

Then it rose gently into the air.
Wilbur didn't wake up.

It flew gently around the room.
Wilbur didn't wake up.

Then it zoomed out of the window.
Wilbur woke up.

'**Meeoow!**' he cried.

Winnie heard him.
She looked up, just in time to see the
flying carpet zoom up into the sky.

'Oh no!' cried Winnie. She grabbed her magic
wand and her broomstick, and zoomed up
into the sky after them.

Winnie flew as fast as her broomstick
could go, but the carpet was faster.
It swooped over the clock tower,
and under a bridge.

Winnie followed it.
'Hang on tight, Wilbur!' she called.
'Meeoow!' cried Wilbur.

Then the carpet flew over a funfair.
What fun!

First it whizzed down the
Roller Coaster Rocket.
Winnie whizzed down behind it.

Then it tried the
Terrible Twister.

The flying carpet was
having a wonderful time.
Wilbur was having a
horrible time.

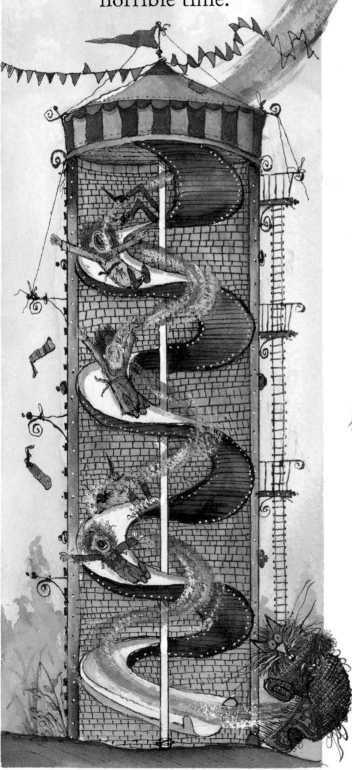

Winnie was worried.
She would never catch them.

Then she had an idea.
She waved her magic wand,
shouted,

Abracadabra!

. . . and everything stopped.

Nothing whizzed or zoomed
or shrieked or splashed.

All was still. Including the flying carpet.

Wilbur jumped onto Winnie's shoulder.
'Purr, purr,' he said.

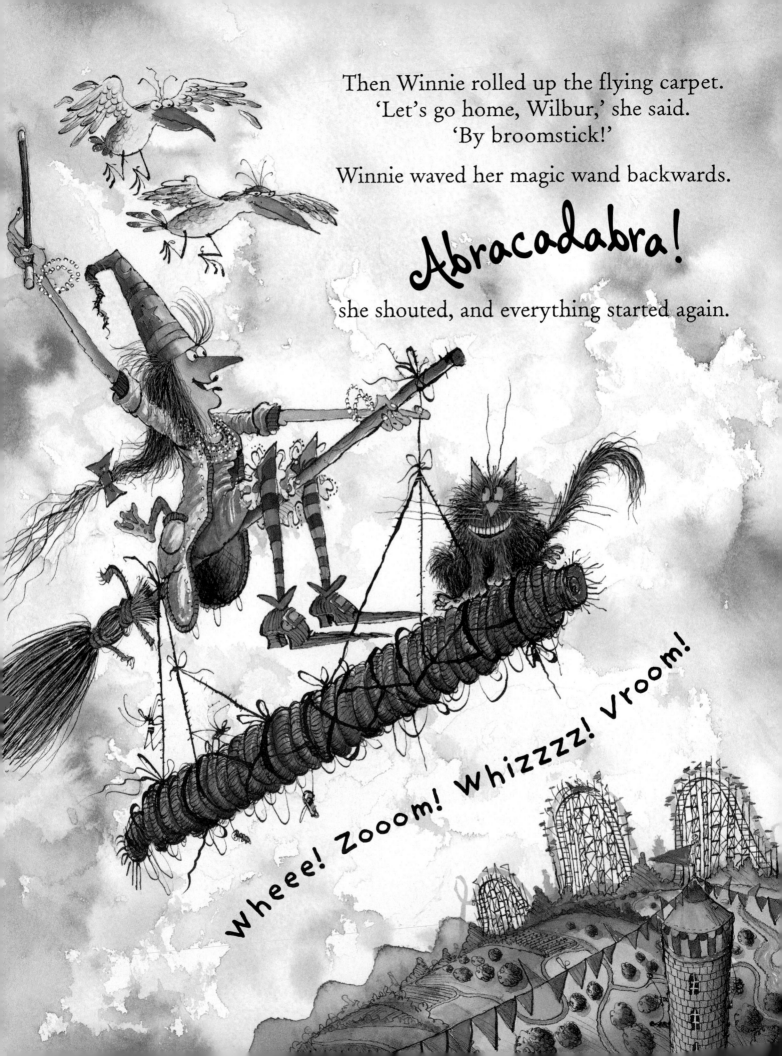

Then Winnie rolled up the flying carpet.
'Let's go home, Wilbur,' she said.
'By broomstick!'

Winnie waved her magic wand backwards.

Abracadabra!

she shouted, and everything started again.

Wheee! Zooom! Whizzzz! Vroom!

Winnie and Wilbur landed in Winnie's garden.
Winnie frowned at the flying carpet.

What would she do with it?

Then Winnie had a wonderful idea.
She shut her eyes,
waved her wand, shouted,

. . . and there, tied to two trees, was a beautiful hammock.

Winnie and Wilbur climbed in. They were both very tired.

The hammock rocked gently in the breeze.

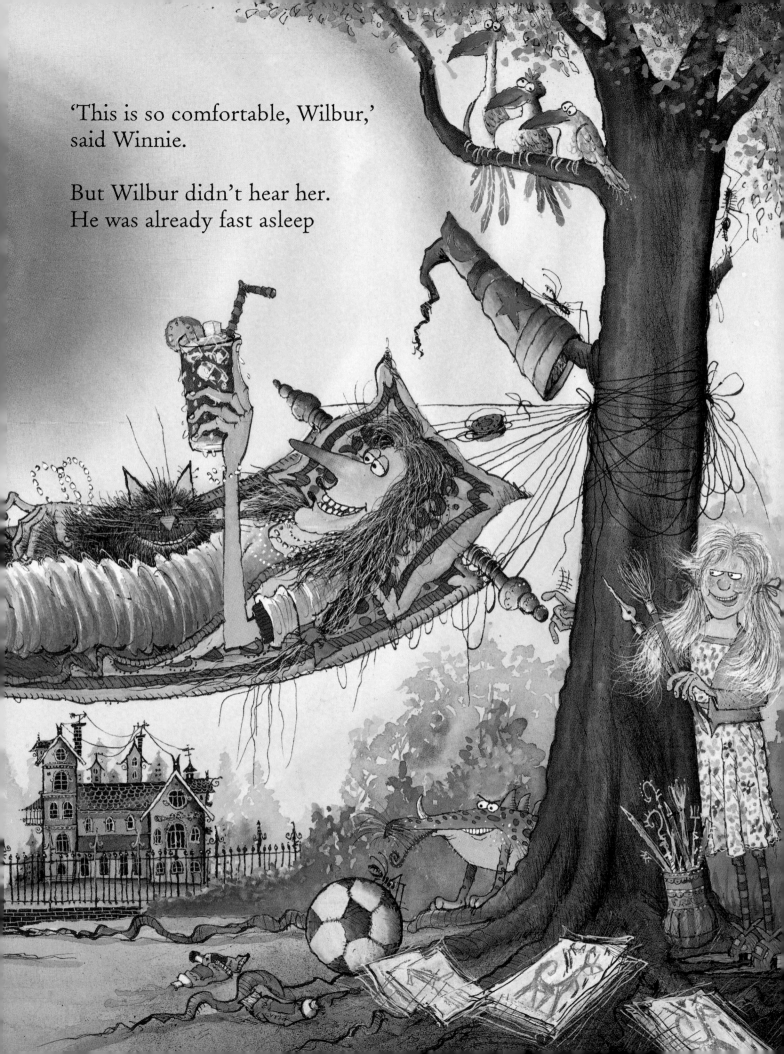

'This is so comfortable, Wilbur,'
said Winnie.

But Wilbur didn't hear her.
He was already fast asleep